This book belongs to

_____

D1303817

Disney's
STORIES FOR ME

Disney's STORIES FOR ME

Edited by Nancy Parent

Illustrated by Disney Storybook Artists

Disney PRESS

NEW YORK

Copyright © 2002 Disney Enterprises, Inc.
All rights reserved.
No part of this book may be reproduced or transmitted in any form or by any means,
electronic or mechanical, including photocopying, recording, or by any information storage
and retrieval system, without written permission from the publisher. For information address
Disney Press, 114 Fifth Avenue, New York, New York 10011-5690.
First Edition
1 3 5 7 9 10 8 6 4 2
ISBN 0-7868-5384-0
For more Disney Press fun, visit www.disneybooks.com

TABLE OF CONTENTS

Walt Disney's Pinocchio

Once upon a time, Geppetto the wood-carver made a special puppet that he named Pinocchio. "I wish you were a real boy," said Geppetto, sadly.

That night the Blue Fairy came to Geppetto's

workshop. "Good Geppetto," she said, "you have made others so happy, you deserve to have your wish come true."

Smiling, the Blue Fairy touched the puppet gently with her wand. "Little puppet made of pine, wake! The gift of life be thine!" And in the blink of an eye, she brought Pinocchio to life.

"Pinocchio, if you are brave, truthful, and unselfish, you will be a real boy someday," said the Blue Fairy.

Then she turned to Jiminy Cricket. "Jiminy," she said, "you must help Pinocchio." She told Jiminy that she was giving him a very important job. He must be Pinocchio's conscience—keeper of the knowledge of right and wrong.

The next day, Geppetto proudly sent his little wooden boy off to school. "Jiminy Cricket will show you the way," said Geppetto. "Be sure to go right there!"

Pinocchio headed off, but never found his way to

school. He went away with Stromboli, an evil puppeteer, who promised to make him famous. That night, Pinocchio had great fun as he danced on the stage. But afterward Stromboli locked him in a cage so he could never escape.

The Blue Fairy appeared and asked Pinocchio why he

hadn't gone to school. Pinocchio lied and told her he had been kidnapped. Suddenly, his nose began to grow.

When Pinocchio finally told the truth, the fairy set him free. "I'll forgive you this once, Pinocchio. But this is the last time I can help you. Remember, a boy who won't be good

might just as well

be made of wood!"

The next day,

Pinocchio met a

man who drove a

stagecoach pulled

by a team of sad little donkeys. "Come with us to

Pleasure Island!" said the coachman. The stagecoach was

full of noisy boys. They were laughing and talking all at

once. Pinocchio thought it looked like fun.

"Don't go, Pinoke!" cried Jiminy Cricket, but still

Pinocchio climbed aboard, ready for adventure.

On Pleasure Island, Pinocchio and the other boys ran wild and stuffed themselves with sweets. But Pinocchio's fun did not last long. All of a sudden, he began to grow donkey ears and a tail!

Pinocchio was frightened. He and Jiminy Cricket ran for their lives, away from Pleasure Island.

But when the two returned home, Geppetto was gone. Pinocchio was very upset. Where could Geppetto be? A dove suddenly appeared with a note from Geppetto. The note said he had gone to sea to look for Pinocchio and had been swallowed by a whale.

Pinocchio set off at once to find Monstro the Whale and save his father. And indeed, Pinocchio found Geppetto in the belly of the great whale. Geppetto was thrilled to see his little puppet. But how were they ever going to get out

of there? Pinocchio had an idea. Together, they built a fire and used the smoke to make Monstro sneeze.

Geppetto and Pinocchio were thrown out of the whale and into the sea. Fighting the waves, Pinocchio helped

get his father to shore safe and sound. But there was

Pinocchio lying facedown in the water! Geppetto

scooped Pinocchio up in his arms and carried him home.

Geppetto laid Pinocchio on his bed and knelt by his side.

"Little Pinocchio, you risked your life to save me," he sobbed.

Suddenly, the Blue Fairy appeared once more. Waving

her magic wand over Pinocchio, she said, "Now you have proved yourself brave, truthful, and unselfish. Today you will become a real boy. Awake, Pinocchio, awake!"

Jiminy Cricket watched as his friend came to life. Their troubles were over, and Jiminy's job was done. At last, Geppetto's wish for a real son had come true.

DISNEY'S STORIES FOR ME

WALT DISNEY'S
Cinderella

Once upon a time, there was a pretty young girl named Cinderella. Cinderella was loved by everyone because she was good and sweet and kind. But Cinderella's widowed father believed she needed a mother. So he got married again to a woman with two

daughters of her own. Soon Cinderella's father died, and she was left to live with her mean stepmother and two jealous stepsisters in the attic of their house.

Poor Cinderella had to do all of the cooking and cleaning. She no longer had nice things and wore only tattered old clothes, while her stepmother and stepsisters had very nice gowns and lived very comfortably.

But no matter how mean her stepmother

and stepsisters were, Cinderella was always cheerful. Even the little animals loved to be near her. She made friends with the mice and birds, making them little outfits to wear and caring for them. Two of Cinderella's best friends were Jaq and Gus. Cinderella and Jaq were always saving Gus

from mean old Lucifer the cat, who had his eye on the plump little mouse.

One day, a letter came,

inviting everyone to the palace for a ball. Cinderella's stepmother said, "Cinderella may go, but only if she finishes her work." Cinderella happily washed, ironed, and scrubbed the floors all day.

Meanwhile, Cinderella's little friends went to work

making her a lovely gown. The birds and mice who loved Cinderella wanted so much to surprise her. And when she saw what they had done, she was very touched. She put on the beautiful dress and ran downstairs to join her stepsisters.

The birds and mice had used sashes and ribbons and beads that belonged to Cinderella's stepsisters to make

the dress look nice. But when her stepsisters saw the gown, they tore it to shreds.

"That's my ribbon!" cried one.

"And those are my beads!" yelled the other.

Cinderella ran to the garden in tears. "Now I can't go to the ball!" she cried.

"Don't cry, child," said a gentle voice. "I am your fairy godmother, and I have come to help you."

Then the Fairy Godmother waved her wand. Four mice became four proud white horses, and a big, round pumpkin became a glittering coach.

Again the Fairy Godmother waved her wand and turned Cinderella's torn dress into a beautiful gown. "You must leave the ball by midnight," she warned. "After that, the magic spell will be broken."

At the ball, the Prince danced with Cinderella all evening. She felt as if she were floating in a dream!

The King and the Grand Duke were delighted to see them falling in love.

But as the clock struck midnight, Cinderella ran from the palace. She was in such a hurry that she left one glass slipper behind. The Prince ran after her, but it was too late.

The next day, the Prince sent the Grand Duke door-to-door to find the young woman who had lost her slipper. When they got to Cinderella's house, both stepsisters tried on the glass slipper, but their feet were much too big.

Cinderella's stepmother told the Grand Duke that there were no other ladies in the house. She had locked Cinderella in her room upstairs on purpose. But Cinderella's little friends Gus and Jaq stole the key from her stepmother's pocket, opened her door, and freed Cinderella just in time.

When Cinderella appeared and asked if she could try on the slipper, her stepmother was furious. She tripped the footman who was holding the slipper on a pillow.

It fell to the floor and shattered.

But Cinderella reached into her apron pocket and pulled out the matching one. It was a perfect fit!

The Grand Duke was happy and relieved that he had found the slipper's owner. The Prince would be married at last. And Cinderella's dreams would all come true.

DISNEY'S STORIES FOR ME

DISNEY'S

THE
LION KING

Everything in the animal kingdom had its place in the circle of life. When the Lion King, Mufasa, and his queen, Sarabi, had a cub named Simba, Mufasa knew that one day Simba would be king. Everyone bowed in respect as Rafiki the baboon introduced the young prince to all the animals.

Only one lion—Mufasa's brother, Scar—refused to attend the ceremony. He was not happy that Simba would be next in line for Mufasa's throne.

But Simba grew into a happy, healthy cub. One day, he proudly told his uncle, "Someday I'm going to rule the whole kingdom! Everything except that shadowy place.

I'm not allowed to go there."

"You're absolutely right, Simba," his uncle agreed slyly.
"Only the bravest lions can go to the elephant graveyard."
Scar deliberately tempted his adventurous nephew.

Simba immediately raced home and convinced his
friend Nala to explore the elephant graveyard. It was

creepier than they had ever imagined.

Zazu, Mufasa's adviser, caught up with the cubs and warned them it was dangerous, too.

But Simba only laughed at Zazu. Then he heard someone laughing back. He turned to see three enemy hyenas ready for lunch. "He's a king fit for a meal," laughed one.

The nasty hyenas

chased the cubs right into a trap. Suddenly, there was a tremendous roar. Mufasa arrived and frightened the hyenas away.

Simba was very proud of his father. "We'll always be together, right?" he asked Mufasa later that evening.

"Look up at the stars, Simba," said Mufasa. "Those are the great kings of the past looking down on us. Remember, those kings will always be there to guide you. So will I."

Although Scar was very angry with the hyenas for letting Simba escape, he made a bargain with them. If they helped him become king, they could have their run of the Pride Lands. And Scar had a plan.

Later Scar brought Simba to a gorge and promised

him a wonderful surprise if he would wait on a certain rock. Then he signaled the hyenas.

The surprise was a stampeding herd of wildebeests! The earth trembled as the wildebeests headed right into the gorge and straight toward Simba. Simba

held onto a tree branch but was slipping fast.

In an instant, Mufasa appeared and grabbed his son. He got Simba to safety, but then he slipped off the ledge and fell into the thundering stampede.

When everything was quiet once more, Simba found his father lying lifeless at the foot of a cliff. Simba had not seen Scar push Mufasa to his death. Simba believed it was all his fault.

"Run away, Simba," Scar advised the young cub. "Run away and never return."

Scar watched as the young cub ran away, chased by

the hyenas. Then Scar returned to Pride Rock and announced to the lions that he would be their new king.

Simba ended up in the desert, where he collapsed from heat and exhaustion. Luckily, two curious creatures found him—a meerkat called Timon and a warthog named Pumbaa.

Simba's new friends took him home to the jungle, where they introduced him to Timon's idea of hakuna matata—"no worries."

Simba tried to put the past behind him, but it was difficult. One day, a young lioness appeared, looking for

When the fighting was over, Simba took his rightful place as king and restored the Pride Lands to a place of peace. And when Simba and Nala's little cub was born, a brand-new circle of life was begun.